Sulley

Mike

Mr Waternoose

Boo

STARRING

Randall

Roz

This edition published by Parragon in 2010
Parragon
Queen Street House
4 Queen Street
Bath, BA1 1HE, UK

ISBN 978-1-4075-9418-7
Printed in China

DISNEY·PIXAR
MONSTERS, INC.

Bath · New York · Singapore · Hong Kong · Cologne · Delhi · Melbourne

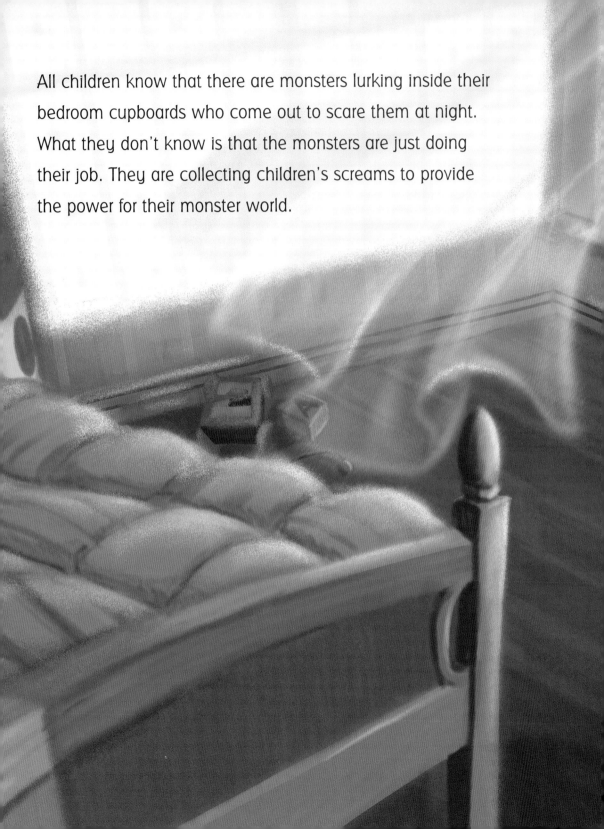

All children know that there are monsters lurking inside their bedroom cupboards who come out to scare them at night. What they don't know is that the monsters are just doing their job. They are collecting children's screams to provide the power for their monster world.

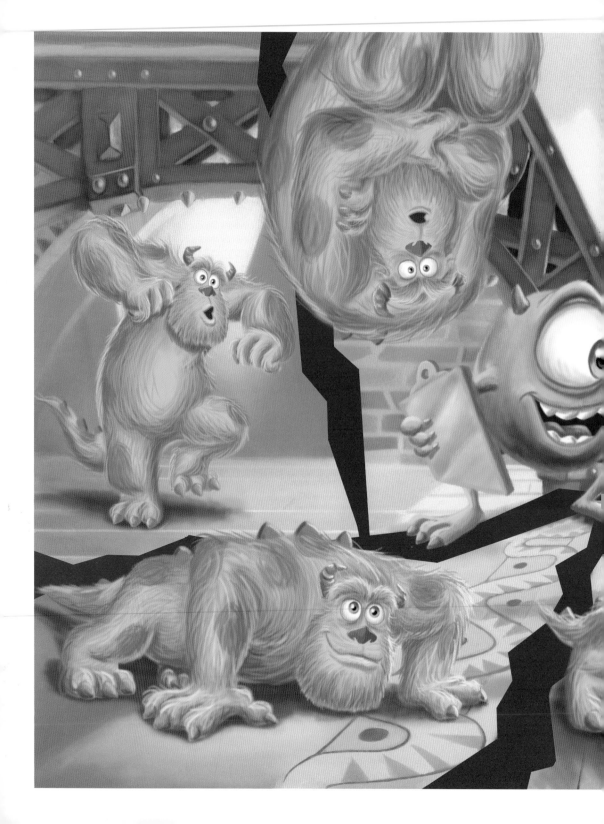

Some of the scariest monsters work for Mr Waternoose, President of Monsters Incorporated, the largest scream-processing factory in the monster world.

James P. Sullivan, the number one Scarer at Monsters, Inc. and his assistant Mike Wazowski, always collect the most screams. Every morning, Mike puts Sulley through vigorous scare training to keep him on top form.

But being a Scarer is a dangerous job. "Never let a kid through one of our doors! Contact with children is deadly!" Mr Waternoose warns his new recruits.

One beautiful morning, since
there was a scream shortage,
Mike and Sulley left the car
at home and walked through
Monstropolis to work.

Mike went to see Roz, the
slug-like monster dispatcher
at Monsters, Inc. She scolded him
for forgetting to file his paperwork, then he
made his way up to the locker room to get ready for work.

Randall, who was not a very nice monster, was already there. He wanted to beat Sulley and become the top Scarer.

"May the best monster win!" said Sulley, cheerfully.

"I plan to!" said Randall, spitefully.

Mike hurried to the Scare Floor with the other assistants and set about ordering up the wardrobe doors for that day, which were used to enter the human world.

Then the Scarers entered the Scare Floor. It was time for business.

The monsters raced in and out of children's rooms, scaring kids and collecting screams. By the end of the day Sulley was top Scarer once again.

With work over, Mike went to meet his girlfriend, Celia, the company's beautiful receptionist. He was taking her to dinner to celebrate her birthday, but he'd forgotten to file his paperwork. Sulley offered to do it for him and went back to the Scare Floor.

He found a child's door
left in its Scaring Station.
Whilst trying to investigate, he
accidentally let a human girl into the monsters' world!

After several failed attempts to return the toxic kid, Sulley
bundled her inside a Monsters, Inc. sports bag. He was just
about to set off to find Mike on his date with Celia, when Randall
appeared acting very suspiciously. Sulley hid with the girl until
he was out of sight. Something strange was going on.

Sulley tracked Mike down and started to explain everything. But while they were distracted, the child crawled out of the bag, scaring all the monsters in the sushi restaurant.

The Child Detection Agency, was alerted and before long agents were swarming overhead in helicopters. In all the confusion, Sulley and Mike managed to grab the girl and escape.

Back at their flat, the two
monsters tried to keep the kid
amused while they figured out
a way to get her back to her world.
When Mike tripped and fell, the little
girl giggled, making all the lights flash
brightly and then go out. This puzzled Sulley.
Her laughter seemed even more powerful than screams.

When she finally grew tired, Sulley tucked her up in his bed.
He was beginning to realize that humans aren't that toxic after all.

The next morning, Sulley decided it would be best to try and put the girl back through her door again. Dressing her in a homemade monster disguise, he and Mike took her to work with them.

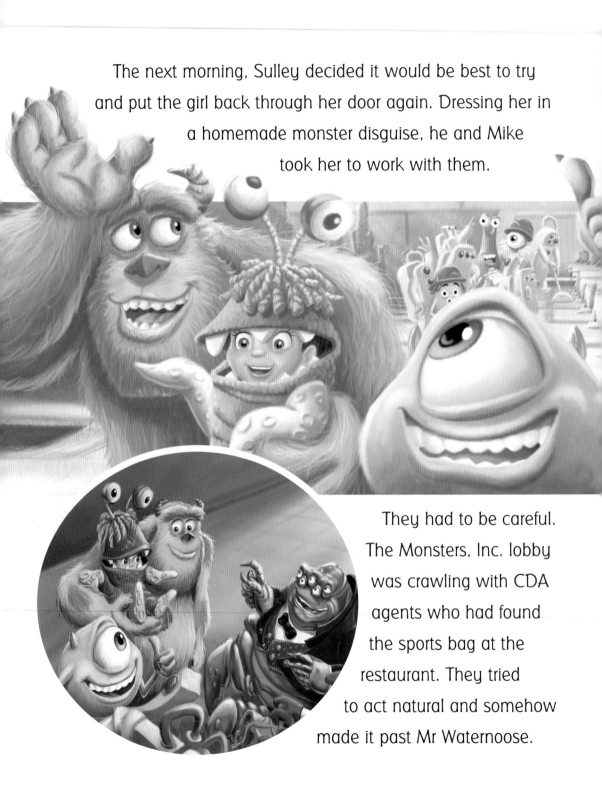

They had to be careful. The Monsters, Inc. lobby was crawling with CDA agents who had found the sports bag at the restaurant. They tried to act natural and somehow made it past Mr Waternoose.

While Mike went to find the key to her door, Sulley and the girl played together in the changing room.

"Boo!" she giggled, running off.

Just as Mike returned to find Sulley and Boo (as Sulley had decided to call her), Randall and his assistant arrived.

"Shhh!" whispered Sulley, as they hid inside a cubicle.

"When I find whoever let that kid out…" muttered Randall.

"This is very bad," said Mike, as he and Sulley just managed to get Boo on to the Scare Floor without being seen. But once again Boo escaped … and Sulley rushed off to look for her.

As Mike tried to apologise to Celia for ruining her evening, he noticed Randall lurking nearby.

But it was too late. Randall had already overheard that Mike and Sulley had been in the same restaurant as the child.

"Where's the kid? It's here in the factory, isn't it?" he growled.

Under threat, Mike had to admit everything. Randall offered to help return the kid. He told Mike to take her to the Scare Floor at lunchtime, when it was empty and he would make sure that Boo's door was ready.

Sulley and Mike eventually found Boo playing with some little monsters in the company crèche. They took her back to the Scare Floor. Mike told Sulley about Randall's plan, but Sulley didn't trust Randall. He was growing fond of Boo and he didn't want anything to happen to her.

Mike thought Sulley was imagining things. He opened Boo's
door and went into her room to prove everything was safe.
He jumped up and down on the bed, pretending to be Boo.
Suddenly, a box was thrown over him and he was trapped inside!

Hiding with Boo, Sulley watched as Randall left the room,
carrying the box. The scheming monster obviously didn't realize
that he had captured Mike, not a kid!

Sulley and Boo followed them, but Randall had disappeared.
Then Boo found a door which led into a secret laboratory.
Randall had strapped Mike to a terrible
machine made to extract screams
from children. Sulley secretly
unplugged the machine and
rescued Mike.

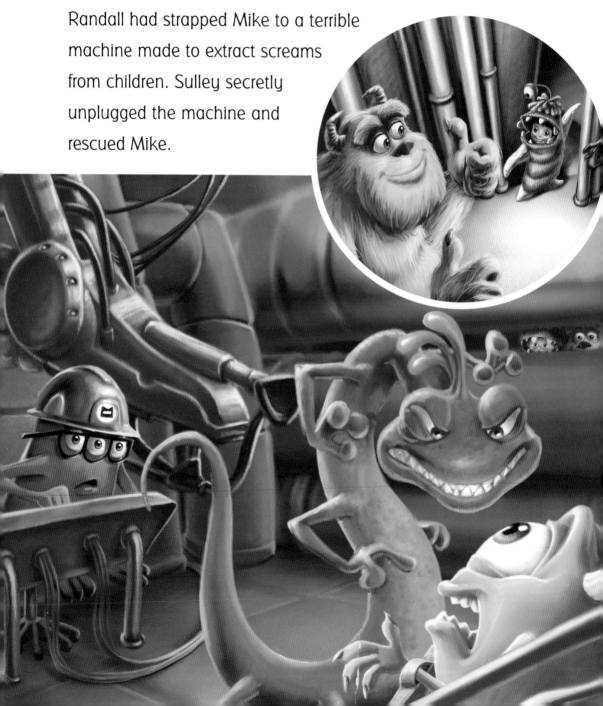

Then they ran to find Mr Waternoose, but as they were trying
to explain to their boss what had happened, he grabbed Boo,
opened a door … and pushed Mike and Sulley through it.
Waternoose was in on Randall's plan!

Waternoose had banished them to the human world. Mike
and Sulley found themselves on a cold and snowy mountainside.

Before long the two monsters bumped into a big, white monster – it was the Abominable Snowman! When he told them about a nearby village, Sulley had an idea. He made a sledge out of bits and pieces he found in the monster's cave. When Mike refused to go with him, Sulley sped down the mountain alone.

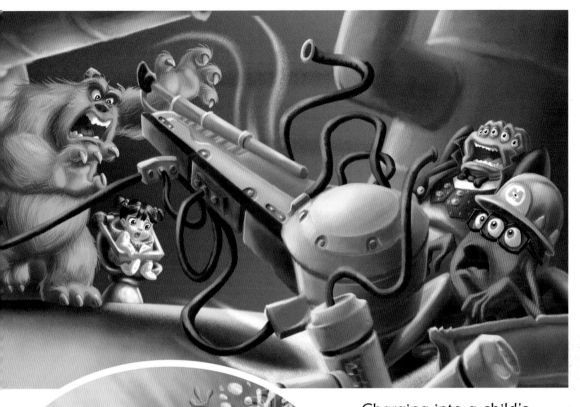

Charging into a child's
bedroom and through
their wardrobe door,
Sulley entered the
monsters' world and raced
towards Randall's secret lab.
He found Boo strapped to the
machine. He ripped the machine apart and freed Boo.

Randall turned invisible and attacked Sulley, but Mike appeared
just in time. He had followed Sulley after all, bringing a supply of
snowballs. He threw one at Randall, making him visible again.

Running to the Scare
Floor, Mike and Sulley
found Boo's door on the
conveyor belt. But Randall
was close behind! Randall grabbed Boo
and tried to loosen Sulley's grip so he would fall. But with Boo's
help, Sulley threw Randall through an open door and quickly put
it through the shredding machine so that he could never return!

With a look of pride, Sulley lifted Boo up into the air and
laughed, "You did it Boo! You beat him!"

Now it was time to escape from Waternoose. "I'll kidnap a thousand children before I let this company die!" he gasped.

But the CDA had heard everything. The agents arrested Waternoose, then announced the arrival of their boss ... who turned out to be Roz! She had been working undercover for the CDA all along!

Roz gave Mike and
Sulley five minutes to
say goodbye to Boo.
Then she would be sent
home and her door would
be shredded so no monster
could ever enter her room again.

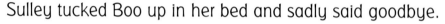

Sulley tucked Boo up in her bed and sadly said goodbye.

Later, when Sulley explained to everyone how Boo's laughter
created more power than her screams, Monsters, Inc. was turned
into a laughter factory. He was made the president and the
company's profits soared.

Sulley still missed Boo. In fact, he was thinking about her when Mike arrived with a surprise for him.

Mike had been busy gluing together all the tiny pieces of Boo's shredded door! Putting the final piece in place, Sulley walked into the room to find Boo waiting with a big smile. At last they were reunited!